Fatal Fangs

"We can't fight her," Watch said, seeming to fall under the spell of Shaetore. The queen of the vampires held out her hand.

"Come to me," she said. "You will go first."

Watch stepped toward her. He moved as if drugged, staggering slightly.

"Watch!" Adam cried.

Yet it was too late. Already Watch stood before the evil queen.

"Raise your chin," Shaetore said, as she leaned toward him and bared her fangs. "There will be pain for only a moment, then you will know a sweetness unimaginable."

Watch clearly could not resist.

He swayed where he stood.

Queen Shaetore bent closer.

Her teeth were inches from the flesh of his throat.

"Watch!" Sally screamed.

Books by Christopher Pike

Available from MINSTREL Books

CHRISTOPHER PIKE

SPOOKSVILLE #19™

NIGHT OF
THE VAMPIRE

A MINSTREL®
BOOK

Published by POCKET BOOKS
New York   London   Toronto   Sydney   Tokyo   Singapore

A MINSTREL PAPERBACK *Original*

A Minstrel Book published by
POCKET BOOKS, a division of Simon & Schuster Inc.
1230 Avenue of the Americas, New York, NY 10020

ISBN: 0-671-00267-8

First Minstrel Books printing November 1997

10 9 8 7 6 5 4 3 2 1

SPOOKSVILLE is a trademark of Christopher Pike

A MINSTREL BOOK and colophon are registered trademarks of
Simon & Schuster Inc.

Cover art by John Youssi

Printed in the U.S.A.

SPOOKSVILLE™ # 19

NIGHT OF THE VAMPIRE

The gang was playing tennis at the town courts Friday after school when the horror with the vampires started. Of course the vampires had been in Spooksville for a while before the gang knew about them, maybe as long as a week. But that unusually warm Friday was their first contact with the ancient enemy.

The gang was Adam Freeman, Sally Wilcox, Cindy Makey, Bryce Poole, and Watch. Tira Jones and George Sanders, who sometimes joined the others, were not around. The gang was playing tennis, doubles—well, sort of, since there were five of them. Adam and Sally were on one team, and the other three made up the other side. The arrangement was thought fair because Watch was half blind and something of a clod when it came to sports. Plus Sally was a fierce competitor. In addition to having long legs and arms, she had a powerful serve and was incredibly coordinated. Sally and Adam had played the others ten games and had won every single one.

"This is getting boring, smashing these guys," Sally said to Adam as she set up to serve. Sally had long dark hair and a mouth that could insult a person just by forming the word *hello*. Yet her sense of humor was refreshing, if one was in an insensitive mood. She had a remarkable wit. Few could match it. Sally continued, "We need to get some real competition."

"Don't get cocky," Adam warned. "They're getting better with each game." Although relatively new to town, Adam was the leader of the group. He was short but had a keen intelligence and was known to risk his life to save others.

"Don't hit it so hard this time," Cindy complained from the other side of the court. Cindy was also new to town. She had long blond hair and was sweet natured—except when she was fighting with Sally. Then she turned into a cat with sharp claws. She was very creative when it came to getting them out of dangerous jams.

"They're allowed to hit it as hard as they like," Bryce told Cindy from beside her. Bryce was handsome, thin, and tall with dark hair. He was also intelligent and brave but had a tendency to rub people the wrong way with his arrogance, especially when he was trying to save the world. But the rest of the group had grown to like him.

"We've got to win at least one game or Sally will never let us live it down," Watch said from behind Cindy and Bryce at the back of the court. Watch had earned his nickname by always wearing four watches, each set to a different time zone. He was perhaps the most brilliant one in the gang but was also very humble and shy. Everyone loved Watch, but no one could say they knew him well. He seemed to live alone, with no family.

"I heard that," Sally said as the court lights came on. "I would say your chances of winning are about as great as my chances of dropping dead in the next five minutes."

"You don't want to say that in this town," Bryce warned.

It was ironic that Ted Tane should stumble onto the court and collapse right then. None of them saw him coming; he just appeared out of the park shadows and fell down near Adam and Sally. The gang was by his side in seconds. They all knew Ted from school. He was their age, twelve, with curly blond hair and wide blue eyes. He played a lot of sports and was pretty popular. The gang had not gone out of their way to bring him into their fold. Since they were so often involved in dangerous situations, they didn't feel it was right to upset the natural childhoods of the other kids at school.

But right then Ted looked about as far from natural as possible. He was stark white and was holding a handkerchief to his neck. Really, they couldn't believe how pale he was; he looked as if he had been carved from marble and brought to life. Yet his life might have been in danger at the moment. As he lay on the asphalt, he writhed from side to side as if lost in a fever. Adam knelt by his side and held him down to get him to lie still. Ted never let go of the handkerchief he had at his neck.

"Ted," Adam said anxiously. "What's wrong? What happened to you?"

Ted did not answer. He became still and stared at Adam with unfocused eyes. His eyes were no longer clear but were bloodshot. Watch also knelt beside the delirious boy. Carefully, Watch reached up and pulled away the handkerchief from Ted's neck.

It was covered with blood.

"He's bleeding!" Cindy said, cringing.

"You're so astute," Sally said. "But why is he bleeding? What's wrong with him?"

"Shaetore," Ted mumbled.

Adam and Watch leaned closer.

"What did you say, Ted?" Adam asked.

"Queen," Ted whispered.

"Who is this queen?" Watch asked.

They could get nothing more out of him. Yet it did look as if Ted had somehow gashed his neck.

"We have to get him to a doctor," Adam said. "To a hospital."

"The doctors in this town all moonlight as undertakers," Sally said. "They don't want anyone to survive. It's better if we take care of him. He's not bleeding too much right now."

"But he's already lost a lot of blood," Watch said gravely. "Look at him, he has his eyes open and doesn't even see us. He's cold and white. I think he needs a transfusion immediately—at least three pints of blood. This is one of the few times when I say the hospital is our only choice."

Sally chewed on that for a moment.

"Then if we are going, let's take him now," she said. "It's not far, just a couple of blocks. We can carry him, if we all work together."

With the guys taking the upper part of Ted's body and the girls taking his legs, they lifted Ted off the ground and started out of the park. The sun had just set, and the shadows cast by the scattered lights seemed darker than usual. Ted had stopped writhing and appeared to have slipped into unconsciousness. His breathing was faint and rapid, and they were worried he would die before they even reached the hospital.

"If he bled so much from that neck wound," Cindy said as they left the park, "why aren't his clothes soaked with blood?"

"I was wondering the same thing myself," Watch said. "The marks on his neck are weird."

"What's weird about them?" Sally demanded.

"They look like teeth marks," Watch said.

It took them fifteen minutes to reach the hospital, Spooksville Memorial, which was painted solid black. Hearses were used as ambulances. The place appeared fairly deserted as they carried Ted inside and up to the front desk of the emergency room. There sat a young nurse with beautiful long black hair and dark red lips. She jumped up when she saw them carrying Ted.

"What happened to him?" she asked with concern.

"We don't know," Adam explained as they gently set Ted down on the floor. Sally fetched a pillow from the waiting room couch and placed it under his head. "We were at the park playing tennis when he stumbled onto the court and collapsed. His neck is bleeding, and he appears to have lost a lot of blood."

The nurse came around the counter and knelt beside Ted, checking his pulse at the neck. Her pretty face wrinkled with worry.

"He is in bad shape," she said, standing suddenly. "I'll get a doctor. Do any of you know the boy's parents?"

"I do, sort of," Cindy said. "I'll call them if you want."

"Do that," the nurse said as she disappeared down the hall.

The gang stayed close to Ted, unsure what to do or say. Cindy was off trying to find a phone. Watch frowned as he continued to study Ted's neck wounds.

"Was he bit by an animal of some kind?" Sally finally asked.

"He was bit by something," Watch said.

Cindy finally returned, looking unhappy.

"No one answers at Ted's house," she said.

"Are you sure you had the right number?" Sally asked.

"I got it from Information," Cindy answered.

"The woman who takes care of Information pulls

7

numbers out of a basket," Sally said. "Did you check the phone book yourself?"

Cindy nodded. "I double-checked the number. There's no one home."

"Maybe this is a case of child abuse," Bryce said. "Maybe the parents have fled the city to escape criminal prosecution."

"Ted's parents didn't bite him," Watch grumbled.

The nurse returned with a doctor and an orderly, and they loaded Ted onto a gurney.

"Do you know what happened to him?" the doctor snapped. He was a man of about sixty with bushy eyebrows and a stern expression. Yet he looked like a doctor, someone who knew what he was doing, and that reassured them somewhat—especially after all Sally's horror stories about the hospital. On the way to the place she would not shut up about the medical experiments they performed on sick patients.

They gave a collective shrug in answer to the doctor's question.

"He just stumbled into our tennis game this way," Adam said.

The doctor frowned. His name tag said Dr. Paine. The nurse's name tag said Sharon RN. She was applying a cuff to check Ted's blood pressure as they talked, and once again Adam could not help noticing how pretty she was. The funny thing was, he thought he had seen her before somewhere. But he couldn't remember precisely where.

"This is the third case like this in the last two days," Dr. Paine muttered under his breath as he drew blood from Ted.

Watch jumped at that. "What do you mean?" he asked.

The doctor had handed the tube of blood to be typed to the orderly and was now wheeling Ted away, the nurse by his side.

"We'll talk later," the doctor called over his shoulder. "We have to save this young man's life. Nurse, prepare for immediate emergency transfusions."

"Yes, Doctor," the nurse said.

They disappeared around a corner. The gang stumbled over to the waiting room chairs and sofas and plopped down. Watch continued to frown.

"What is it?" Sally asked, studying him.

Watch shrugged. "Nothing."

But it was clear it was something.

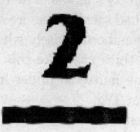

2

As it turned out, they didn't get to see Ted again that night. The nurse finally came out three hours later and said that Ted's condition had been stabilized but that he was too weak to talk. The nurse asked for Ted's phone number, and Cindy gave it to her. Then the gang walked home together.

But along the way they stopped at Ted's house.

They rang the doorbell a dozen times.

There was no one home, even though it was late.

The next day, Saturday, they were all up early and at the hospital. Yet they had to wait a long time before they were allowed in to see Ted. The nurse from the previous night was gone, but Dr. Paine was still on duty. He looked exhausted. Watch quizzed him as they were led to Ted's room.

"You said this was the third case like this in the last two days," Watch said. "What did you mean?"

"Exactly what I said," the doctor replied. "In the last forty-eight hours I've had a man and a young woman come into the hospital in the same condition as your friend."

"What exactly was Ted's condition?" Watch asked.

Dr. Paine paused outside a closed hospital room.

"Your friend was suffering from a massive loss of blood," he said. "I can't put it any more simply."

"What about the wounds on his neck?" Watch asked.

Dr. Paine frowned. "What wounds?"

"He had a couple of gash marks on his neck when we brought him in," Sally explained. "Didn't you stitch them up? That's where he was bleeding from."

"I didn't see any marks on his neck," Dr. Paine replied, puzzled. "I had no idea how he had lost so much blood."

"Is Ted better now?" Cindy asked.

"He's still very weak," Dr. Paine said, reaching for the doorknob. "He has also developed a severe intolerance of sunlight. Don't open the blinds while you're talking to him."

Watch and Sally jumped slightly at this last piece of news.

They went inside the room to see Ted.

He was sitting up as they entered, propped up by a mound of pillows. At first glance he just looked a little tired, but a closer examination showed that his eyes were still bloodshot and the pallor of his skin had not brightened despite the transfusions he had received. But it was hard to see him very clearly. As Dr. Paine had said, all the curtains were drawn and the room was rather dark.

The room was also strangely cool.

Dr. Paine left them alone to talk to Ted.

"How are you feeling?" Cindy asked anxiously, taking Ted's hand. She cringed slightly at the touch. Cindy was surprised by the coldness of his skin. Ted looked at her with dazed eyes.

"I feel good," he said weakly.

"You look horrible," Sally remarked. "What happened to you?"

Ted stared at Sally as if seeing her for the first time.

"What do you mean?" he asked.

"I mean, how did you lose a gallon of blood?" Sally said. "And who was chewing on your neck?"

Ted just kept staring at her, not blinking once.

"I don't know what you're talking about," he said.

"You have no memory of what happened last night?" Bryce asked.

"No," Ted said flatly.

"Do you remember stumbling onto the tennis court?" Adam asked.

"No," Ted said.

"What do you remember?" Watch asked.

"I told you, I remember nothing," Ted said.

"Then what is the last thing you remember?" Sally persisted.

Ted's tone grew cold. "Why are you asking me all these questions?"

"We just want to understand what happened to you," Cindy said, still holding his hand. "We're worried about you."

"Don't be," Ted said curtly. "I'm fine."

"You're far from fine," Sally said, stepping closer. "You're in a hospital because you've lost massive amounts of blood." She leaned over the bed and studied his neck. "Where are the marks on your neck?"

"I don't know what you're talking about," Ted said.

"I bet you don't," Sally said, suddenly retreating

to the window. In a single swift move, she threw open the curtains. Ted literally howled in pain. His whole body spasmed, and he rolled up into a ball as he threw the blanket over his head.

"Sally!" Cindy cried. "Close that curtain! You heard what Dr. Paine said. Sunlight is bad for Ted right now."

Sally closed the curtain and stepped back to the bed. Slowly Ted uncovered his head and looked around. His bloodshot eyes blazed with anger. Yet the expression did not bother Sally. A look of smug understanding filled her face.

"But why does sunlight bother our dear Ted?" Sally asked quietly.

Watch interrupted. "Ted, I think we need to leave you right now, let you rest. We'll check on you later and see how you're doing, OK?"

Ted fought to control his anger, to hide it perhaps.

"I won't be here when you come back," he said.

Cindy squeezed his hand. "You rest and get well."

At Watch's prodding, the gang left the room.

They talked outside in the hallway.

"He's a vampire," Sally said with absolute authority. "There's no question about it. We have to make a wooden stake and drive it through his heart. Then we have to cut off his head, stuff his mouth full of garlic, and sink his body in a pond of fresh water." She paused to catch her breath. "I can't stand vampires."

Now Cindy appeared in shock. "Huh?" she said.

"That's ridiculous," Adam said. "Ted is sick, that's all. We're not sticking anything through his heart."

"You're so weird," Cindy said to Sally, scowling.

Watch spoke reluctantly. "I'm afraid I agree with Sally."

Adam and Cindy stared at him in shock.

"You can't be serious," Adam muttered.

Watch was uncomfortable. "I'm not talking about hammering a stake through Ted's heart this very minute. But he's definitely showing signs of prevampiric syndrome."

Cindy frowned. "What's that?"

"Ted isn't a vampire yet," Watch said. "Not completely. But he's well on his way. By tonight he'll probably be out sucking the blood out of half the town."

"Better to destroy him now before others are contaminated," Sally said matter-of-factly.

"But we go to school with Ted," Cindy cried. "We can't just kill him."

Adam comforted her. "No one's going to kill

anybody. There has to be an explanation for all this. Watch, how can you be sure you're right?"

Watch shrugged. "He has all the classic signs. His neck was cut open last night. Now the wounds have vanished. He cannot bear the sun. And he obviously had a huge amount of blood drained from his veins." Watch paused. "A powerful vampire must have attacked him shortly before we saw him. Remember, it was dark by then."

"But where did this vampire come from?" Adam asked.

"Maybe it is one of the vampire girls who work at the theater," Sally suggested.

Watch waved the idea away. "Those girls only pretend to be vampires. They're not the real thing. No, what got hold of Ted is in a different league. I just wonder how many others in town have been infected."

"We know of at least two others," Bryce said, referring to Dr. Paine's other two patients. "We have to check on them before we leave the hospital."

"Good idea," Watch said. "But more important, we have to find the hiding place of the vampires while it is still daylight. Once the sun goes down, we won't be able to stand against them."

"Wait a second," Adam said. "I want to talk

about this some more. I still don't believe we have real vampires in town."

"Then test Ted," Watch said. "Find some garlic, bring it into his room, and see how he reacts."

"Or see if you can see his reflection in a mirror," Sally said. "I bet it's fading already."

"There's a mirror in his room," Cindy said, not believing a word of what they were saying. She reached for the door to Ted's room. "I'll look at him in it and prove to you that you're crazy."

Adam stopped her. "Wait. I'll go with you."

"Why?" Cindy asked. "He's sick, he isn't going to hurt me."

"If he's a vampire, he could kill you," Sally said darkly. "Or worse."

"We'll check him out together," Adam told Cindy as he carefully opened the door. In the short time they had talked in the hallway, it appeared as if Ted had fallen asleep. He lay on his back with his face partly covered by the sheet. Adam and Cindy quietly stepped to the far side of the bed so that they had his and their reflections in the mirror.

Only they couldn't see Ted's head in the mirror.

"Oh no," Adam gasped softly.

"We can't see him because he's got his head covered," Cindy whispered.

"It's not covered up that much," Adam whispered back. "We should at least be able to see his hair."

"You're not saying you believe those guys?" Cindy demanded.

"I'm beginning to believe them," Adam admitted.

Cindy was a mass of nerves. "We can't hurt Ted."

"I'm not saying we have to hurt him," Adam said. "Come on, let's get out of here."

The others were waiting in the hallway.

"I guess you're over your doubts," Sally said, reading their expressions.

"It proves nothing," Cindy said quickly. "And you're not hammering a stake through his heart."

"I'll do it," Bryce said.

"He's a bloodsucker," Sally agreed. "He has to die. The sooner the better."

Cindy sulked. "You guys are horrible."

Watch intervened. "No one has to die right now except the vampire or vampires who changed Ted. As I said, we have to find them while the sun is still up."

"But where could they be hiding?" Adam wondered out loud.

"In a dark and secret place," Sally said. "Spooks-

ville is full of them. They could be almost anywhere."

"Why don't we talk to Dr. Paine about the other
two patients right now?" Bryce suggested. "He
might give us a clue about where they're hiding."

The others agreed that that was a good idea.

They found Dr. Paine in the hospital laboratory
studying a blood sample. They could only guess it
was from either Ted or one of the other blood-loss
patients. Dr. Paine glanced up from his microscope
as they entered.

"You kids shouldn't be in here," he said.

"We just wanted to ask a couple of questions
before we leave," Watch said, and gestured to the
microscope. "What are you examining?"

"The lab technician asked me to look at a blood
sample from your friend," Dr. Paine said with a
frown. He turned back to the eyepiece on the
microscope. "He has some unusual blood."

"That's because he's a vampire," Sally said
casually.

Dr. Paine glanced back up. "He's something out
of the ordinary, that's for sure."

"Why do you say that?" Watch asked.

Dr. Paine was puzzled. He stared off into the
distance as he replied.

"Ted's blood seems to have developed an amazing ability to destroy any virus or bacteria that it comes in contact with. It also has a very fast clotting rate. Plus—and this should be impossible—it has almost no salt in it."

"But you need salt to live," Bryce said.

"Vampires are not technically alive," Sally muttered.

"Why did you run all these tests on his blood?" Watch asked the doctor.

Dr. Paine sighed. "I'm searching for answers. I can't get blood samples from the other two patients who lost blood."

"Why not?" Bryce asked. "Where are they?"

"They left last night, in the middle of the night. They didn't even check out."

"What were their names?" Watch asked.

"I'm sorry," Dr. Paine said, "that's confidential information."

"But you can only help them if you get in touch with them," Sally said. "We might be able to help you do that. For their sakes, you should tell us."

Dr. Paine considered for a moment.

"Very well," he said. "I will tell you on the condition that you try to talk them into coming back into the hospital. There are many tests I'd like to run on them. They shouldn't have been able to get up and walk out of here."

"I suspect Ted will do the same thing tonight," Sally muttered.

Dr. Paine ignored her comment, as he had her other remarks about vampires. Apparently Dr. Paine had not seen enough of Spooksville outside the hospital walls to be a true believer. But he did provide them with the names of the other two patients: Kathy Melon and Darrel Fraser. Watch immediately hit upon a connection between them and Ted Tane. But he waited until they were outside to tell the others what it was.

"The Tanes and Melons and Frasers all live out by the old warehouse on Trumbell," Watch said. "That's at the north end of town, near the road that leads up into the mountains. The warehouse there has been deserted for years, but it used to be a foam rubber factory. It could be a perfect place for vampires to sleep during the day."

Sally nodded. "And if they did venture out at night, they might not go too far until their numbers were great. I'm sure some of them must be hiding there."

"Let's remember what Ted mumbled when we first saw him last night," Watch said. "Something about a queen. Shaetore, I think he said. It's possible this queen is the head of the vampires, and the original source of them."

"We need a plan," Bryce said. "We can't just walk into the warehouse and expect to survive. We need holy water, crucifixes, garlic, white roses, wooden stakes—all the things vampires hate."

"I didn't know they hated white roses," Sally muttered.

Cindy was upset. "We can't just walk into that warehouse and start hammering stakes into the chests of people sleeping there. They could just be homeless people."

"There are no homeless in Spooksville except Bum," Sally said. "They've all been exterminated by the other evil creatures that roam our streets after dark."

"Cindy," Watch said patiently. "We'll make sure they're vampires before we start anything. But I think Bryce is right, we must be prepared. I suggest we go to Bryce's house now and make suitable weapons."

"I have plenty of lumber stored up for just such an emergency," Bryce said.

Watch paused. "Cindy, you have to stay away from Ted for now."

Cindy was uneasy. "But you're not going to hurt

him, are you?" she asked for what seemed the tenth time.

"He's a goner, you may as well accept it," Sally said.

"I say waste him now," Bryce said. "He'll be one less vampire to worry about."

"He's flunking math at school anyway," Sally agreed.

"Oh brother," Adam muttered.

"We'll only hurt him if he tries to hurt us," Watch said to Cindy.

Cindy did not relax. "He hasn't done anything to anybody."

"Not yet," Sally said darkly.

3

At Bryce Poole's house they got to work constructing and gathering the tools they thought they'd need to destroy the vampires. But they were at a disadvantage because they had no idea how many of the enemy there were. They briefly discussed sending over someone to check out the situation.

"Good intelligence is everything in this kind of operation," Sally said.

"Then you should go to the warehouse ahead of us," Cindy said.

"Because I am the most intelligent?" Sally asked.

"Because you are the most expendable," Cindy said.

"I think it's a bad idea," Adam said. "We're stronger when we're all together. We hit the warehouse as a group, or we don't hit it at all."

"I wish we had a flame thrower," Bryce said. "It would be the ideal weapon."

"Can't we get one from Mr. Patton's army surplus store?" Watch asked.

Bryce shook his head. "Patton's off on some military exercise. He's part of a secret team training to deal with alien invaders. He won't be back till next week."

"We could break into his shop," Sally suggested. "I'm sure he wouldn't mind."

"We can't do it," Bryce said. "He keeps the place heavily booby-trapped. We'd be blown to pieces."

"Where are we going to get holy water?" Adam asked. "Is there a priest in town?"

"There was, but he was turned into a rabbi by our dear sweet town witch, Ann Templeton," Sally said. "The guy won't eat bacon anymore."

"Why did she do that to him?" Adam asked.

"She went to confession at his church, and then she got mad at him because he didn't take her confession seriously," Watch said. "Even when she told him about all the people she had turned into wild animals, he thought she was joking."

"He doesn't think she's funny now," Sally added.

"We'll have to do without the holy water," Bryce said, holding up a wooden stake he had just fashioned on his high-tech power lathe. "Personally, I prefer hard-core weapons."

"How many stakes should we bring?" Sally asked.

"Four each," Watch said. "And hammers. Do you have garlic, Bryce?"

"No," Bryce said. "But we can stop at the health food store on the way to the warehouse. Of course, we can't buy any of the improved odorless kind that they sell."

"What about the salt angle?" Adam said. "Why would a vampire's blood have no salt?"

"They're probably allergic to it, like the garlic," Watch said. "Salt is used in many ancient traditions to ward off evil. We may as well pick up some rock salt while we're at it."

"Let's get a few flares as well," Bryce said. "They might flee from the fire."

"But aren't vampires supposed to be asleep during the day?" Adam asked. "I was hoping they weren't going to put up a fight."

"They may be asleep now," Watch said. "But I'm

pretty sure they'll wake up when we try to drive stakes through their hearts."

"I bet Ted would wake up," Sally muttered.

"Shut up!" Cindy snapped at her.

Sally just shrugged and looked away.

Bryce fingered the tip of the stake he was holding.

Everyone knew what he was thinking.

They had started the day early, but by the time they reached the warehouse it was close to three in the afternoon. Because it was fall and the days were short, they had cut things pretty tight. Sunset was less than two hours away.

The warehouse at the edge of town was old and ugly. It didn't look as if it had been used in decades, although Watch said the senior class had rented it to host a prom a few years back.

"They cleaned out part of it and hung lights from the ceiling," Watch said. "But they couldn't get rid of the lingering smell of polyurethane. The prom queen ended up getting sick and throwing up just as she was being crowned."

"She actually threw up on the prom king," Sally said.

"What's polyurethane?" Cindy asked.

"Foam rubber," Bryce said. "It's highly flammable."

"Is there much foam rubber left in this place?" Sally asked.

"Tons," Watch said. "But it is heavily decayed."

"But still highly flammable," Sally said.

They were all thinking the same thing. Just set the place on fire and take off. It sure sounded easier than entering the warehouse and searching for monsters. Even in daylight the place had a forbidding air. It was almost as if it were cloaked in a black cloud. Adam felt a chill just staring at the place. Yet he was the first to speak of their unspoken plan.

"We can't do it," he said. "It would be morally wrong to destroy such a large piece of property without good reason."

"I agree," Watch said. "And we need to confront these creatures to see if they are vampires, and to get an idea of how widespread the threat from them is. They may be hiding inside here, but they might be hiding other places as well."

Sally gripped her stakes and flashlight.

"Let's get it over with," she said. "I'll feel better when I've killed a few of those monsters."

"You are brutal," Cindy scolded her.

"I'm a realist," Sally replied. "You have to be if you want to survive in this town."

All the doors were locked. They had to break in, through a window in the rear. The sound of the glass shattering worried them. Had they alerted the enemy? Were they walking into an elaborate trap?

Inside it was dark and dusty. Virtually no sunlight came through the painted windows. They had to turn on a flashlight to take a single step forward. They were in the main body of the warehouse, but the beams from their lights couldn't pierce to the far end. They could see rows of metal shelves, where the foam rubber had been stored before being shipped out. There were also stacks of the aged mattresses themselves. But as Watch had said, these were old and crumbling.

The smell of foam rubber filled the air.

Layered on top of it was another smell—the foul stench of decay.

It seemed to waft up from in front of them.

"I think they're here," Sally whispered.

"Yeah," Watch said, peering around through his thick glasses. "But where?"

"If I were a vampire," Bryce said, "I'd bury myself under a pile of foam rubber."

"If I were a vampire, I'd have a suite at the finest

hotel in town," Sally said. "And my own personal gold-inlaid coffin for daytime naps."

"Thank goodness you're not a vampire," Cindy muttered.

"We can't go through every pile of foam rubber in this place," Adam said. "That would take us until long after the sun set."

Watch considered. "But there is that weird smell. Let's move to where it's strongest and then search the piles there."

They crept through the massive warehouse a long time before finding the spot where the odor was definitely strongest. The problem was, there were dozens of stacks of foam rubber there. They didn't know which one to attack first.

"We could be surrounded by vampires," Sally whispered.

"Or there could be none here," Bryce said. "But just in case, I wish I had a flame thrower."

"We have to work with what we have," Watch said, nodding to a pile of foam rubber off to their right. "Let's just knock this one down and see what we find," he whispered.

"But what if a vampire jumps out and eats us?" Cindy asked.

"It won't eat us," Sally said. "It'll just suck all

our blood. Then we'll be condemned for the rest of eternity to wander every night as a creature of darkness and evil. Our thirst for blood never sated; our fangs forever dripping." Sally paused. "But I thought you didn't believe in this latest plague of vampires?"

"I could believe in almost anything in here," Cindy said quietly.

The others understood. The air around them seemed filled with evil shapes. It was as if while the vampires dreamed their dark thoughts choked the atmosphere.

As a group they lined up on one side of the stack Watch had pointed out, their hands and arms pressed against the foam rubber, their legs braced for a big push. On the count of three they gave it all they had.

The stack wavered and then toppled. A cloud of dust and fumes flew into their faces. For a moment they were all blinded and choking. Polyurethane was particularly hard on the lungs. It took them a whole minute before any of them could see.

Then all at once they could make it out. The vampire.

He lay on his back, dressed entirely in black.

His skin as white as Ted's had been.

His face as lifeless as that of a wax figure.

"He looks dead," Adam gasped.

"Don't be fooled," Sally whispered. "He's merely sleeping."

"Can he hear us?" Cindy wanted to know.

"Give him a shake and ask him," Sally said.

"I'm not touching him," Cindy said.

"I don't want to touch him, either," Adam admitted.

"We have to harden our hearts," Bryce said, lifting a wooden stake. "We must complete our job. Sally, I'll hold the stake over his heart, you pound it in."

Now Sally was having doubts.

"I think Watch should pound it in," she said. "He's stronger than I am."

"Sally's tough except when we need her to be," Cindy muttered.

"I heard that!" Sally snapped. "I don't see you stepping forward to pound in the stake."

"Yeah, but at least I admit that I don't have the stomach for it," Cindy said. "I don't walk around like the Legendary Vampire Killer of Transylvania."

Sally paused and eyed the creature.

"I just don't want him to bite me," Sally muttered.

"Look," Watch said. "Standing in front of a

vampire is the last place we should be having this argument. Bryce, I'll help you pound in the stake. The rest of you stand back. If he should wake up, I want there to be fewer targets."

"I'll stand by you both," Adam said. "If he does wake up, I'll hold a burning torch in his face."

"That's a brave boy," Sally said, retreating a few steps.

The three boys crept forward. The vampire lay on the foam about three feet off the ground. His eyes were closed, and his arms were folded over his chest. They would have to move them to get the stake into the heart. A man of about forty human years, he didn't look familiar to any of them. They suspected he was a vampire the queen had brought with her. Perhaps he was centuries old—they had no way of knowing. There was something haunting in his still expression. He looked as if he had witnessed unimaginable horrors.

Or caused such horrors.

Bryce reached out to pull the vampire's arms aside.

Watch stopped him. "Use the stake to move his arms," he advised. "We don't want to touch him unless we have to."

"Good idea," Bryce said, sliding the point of the stake under the vampire's elbows. Bryce lifted the

33

creature's arms, and they flopped to his sides. If the vampire knew what was happening, he gave no sign. Soon Bryce had the chest area clear. Yet Bryce trembled as he raised the stake above the vampire's heart, and there wasn't a living soul in the warehouse who could blame him. It was grim work, this vampire hunting. But somebody had to do it, and they all knew they were best qualified.

Bryce allowed the tip of the stake to touch the vampire's black shirt.

Still the vampire gave no sign he was about to be impaled.

"Ready?" Watch asked Bryce. Watch raised the hammer.

Bryce nodded. His face was tense.

"Don't hit my hands," Bryce said.

"Don't shake the stake," Watch replied as he raised the hammer higher.

"Do it," Adam whispered, standing ready with his flare.

Watch brought the hammer down.

It never reached the stake.

The vampire suddenly came to life.

He grabbed the stake and twisted it to one side. As a result the blow from Watch's hammer landed straight on the monster's chest, which seemed to hurt even the vampire. He opened his mouth and flashed his sharp fangs at them. At the same time he grabbed both of Bryce's hands. Bryce uselessly tried to struggle free as the vampire sat up and bent his mouth toward Bryce's neck.

Watch smashed his hammer down on top of the vampire's head.

It stunned the monster but only momentarily.

"Quick, Adam!" Watch yelled. "Light the flare!"

Adam couldn't find a place to strike it. He was literally surrounded by stacks of mushy foam rubber. Then he remembered the floor. But it wasn't easy for him to bend over in front of the vampire. Especially when it seemed he was about to bite Bryce's head off.

But bend over Adam did, and in a moment he had the flare blazing. Showing incredible courage, Adam rammed the flare right in the vampire's face. The creature let go of Bryce and howled in agony.

Then he grabbed at Adam.

Watch hit him again on the head with the hammer.

"Throw the flare on the foam rubber!" Watch shouted. "Burn it!"

Adam did as he was told.

Just as the vampire grabbed for his wrists.

Polyurethane really was very flammable.

The old mattress instantly went up in flames.

The group jumped back as the vampire tried to stand and escape the flames. But the fire had already engulfed his supposedly immortal body. Stumbling, the vampire groped toward them. But then he lost his footing and fell back on the pile of burning foam rubber.

Black smoke poured up to the ceiling, and they began to choke.

"We have to get out of here!" Watch shouted. "This whole place is going up in flames!"

As a group they ran toward the window they had entered through. Before they could reach it, pile upon pile of foam rubber caught fire behind them. The interior of the warehouse was turned into a cavern of poisonous fumes. Flames as tall as trees licked at the ceiling. Cindy began to faint, and Adam had to grab her and push her through the open window.

Soon enough they were outside in the fresh air. Each of them stood bent over and coughing as the flames reached the exterior walls of the warehouse. The heat was so intense—they had to back off two hundred yards to keep from getting singed. Yet Sally and Bryce appeared happy.

"We did it," Sally said.

"Nothing, not even a vampire, could survive those flames," Bryce agreed.

Adam turned to Watch, who stared at the burning warehouse with an uneasy expression. "What is it?" Adam asked.

"If there is a vampire queen," Watch said, "she's probably very ancient. I don't believe someone so old could be destroyed so easily."

"There's no reason to think there are more of them," Sally said.

"I disagree," Watch said. "I think there is every reason to think there are more."

"What should we do?" Adam asked.

Watch sighed as he removed his glasses and cleaned them on his shirt.

"Get some expert advice," he said.

4

They tried to find Bum, good old Bum, who used to be town mayor before he was cursed by their resident witch, Ann Templeton. But he was no-where to be found, so they discussed turning to the witch herself.

"But she told us we had to get out of the habit of running to her every time we got in trouble," Adam said.

"The whole town is in trouble," Bryce said. "This is not our personal problem. I think she'll help us."

"She might help us defeat the vampires and then turn us into toads," Sally warned.

"She doesn't do stuff like that," Adam said.

"It's getting dark," Cindy said. "I don't want to go to the witch's castle at night."

"But if there are more vampires running around town," Watch said, "the witch's castle might be one of the few safe places. I'm sure she has the power to resist them."

"I wouldn't count on it," Sally said.

"Let's vote," Adam suggested. "All in favor of going to see Ann Templeton, say aye."

Watch and Bryce immediately said aye. Adam, after a moment's hesitation, also added his positive vote. Sally shook her head. Cindy yawned as if she were exhausted.

"I want to go home," Cindy said. "I think we got all the vampires, and I've had enough excitement for one day."

"We definitely have not got all the vampires," Bryce said. "Remember Ted."

"You promised to leave him alone!" Cindy snapped.

"I don't remember ever making such a promise," Sally muttered.

Watch raised a hand. "We will leave Ted alone if you promise not to go near him, Cindy. Agreed?"

Cindy lowered her head. "OK."

Adam patted her on the back. "The fumes really got to you, didn't they?"

Cindy glanced at him. "It wasn't just the fumes. It was seeing that creature die. It was in such pain."

"Better him than us," Sally said.

"Go home and rest," Adam told Cindy. "We'll catch up with you later."

Cindy nodded and took off in the direction of her house.

The rest of them headed for the witch's castle.

Ann Templeton was waiting for them.

She answered the door of her castle wearing a sweeping purple robe. Her long black hair was hanging loose down her back, and her clear green eyes sparkled with mysterious power. As always, in Adam's opinion, she looked incredibly beautiful. With a brief smile and a nod she led them into a room with stone walls. In the center of the room was a long wooden table; a giant fireplace with crackling logs filled one whole wall. The light from the fire cast an eerie red glow over the entire room. She bid them sit down and have something to drink. Red liquid shimmered in shiny gold chalices. There were four chalices in all. The witch was not drinking with them.

"Don't worry," she said when she saw their hesitation. "It isn't blood."

"What is it?" Watch asked.

"Red Kool-Aid," Ann Templeton said.

They drank the liquid, which indeed turned out to be Kool-Aid.

They hoped.

"I guess you know why we're here," Adam said.

"I suppose I do," she said. "But you can tell me anyway."

They related their tale of the vampires, starting with Ted's bloody stumble onto their tennis court and ending with the destruction of the old warehouse. Ann Templeton listened closely, and when they finished she frowned.

"You're leaving out one point," she said. "This Ted mumbled something to you last night before he lost consciousness. What was it?"

"He said *Shaetore,* Watch said. "Then the word *queen.* We assumed he meant that the queen of the vampires is Queen Shaetore."

Ann Templeton's frown changed to a grimace.

"Shaetore," she whispered. And even the powerful witch seemed momentarily frightened. A tremor passed through her body, but she quickly mastered it. She glanced at all of them and added, "This battle is far from over. Shaetore did not perish in the flames at the warehouse."

"How can you be sure?" Sally asked.

"She wouldn't hide in such an obvious place," the witch explained. "She's crafty, this vampire.

The shadow of her legend is long and red. She is hiding where you'd least expect to see her." Ann Templeton paused, and her gaze was distant. "Also, I feel her near."

"Where?" Adam asked.

The witch shook her head. "I can't say exactly. Shaetore has the power to hide her mind and body from all mortals, myself included. But I do know that she is still in town, and that she will seek revenge for what you have done."

"How do you know her?" Watch said.

"In my witch circles she is well known," Ann Templeton explained. "Shaetore is very old and has been alive—if you can call her vampiric existence life—since the days of Atlantis. She was the first and therefore the most powerful of all vampires. All the legends of such creatures spring from her alone."

"Was she always a vampire?" Adam asked.

"You mean, was she born a vampire?" Ann Templeton asked. "No, that would not have been possible. Vampires do not have children, not in the usual sense. Shaetore was born like any other baby girl. But how she became a vampire is a dark tale indeed. I hesitate to tell it now, knowing that she will soon be walking the streets outside our very doors."

SPOOKSVILLE

"But we need to know all we can about her if we are to defeat her," Watch said.

"Besides, we like a good scary story," Sally said.

Ann Templeton was thoughtful. Once more she stared off into the distance. But perhaps it was off in time and not in space. Her features took on a soft but sad expression.

"I would call Shaetore's tale more tragic than scary," Ann Templeton said finally. "It starts with her mother, Princess Kiel. She was married to Prince Rankte and was the queen of all Atlantis. Her great sadness was that she could not give her husband a male heir to inherit the kingdom when their time came to pass on their crowns. Princess Kiel had twelve children, each one a girl. And each time she had a girl, she cursed the universe for cursing her—never a wise thing to do. Then, the thirteenth time she got pregnant, she delivered still another girl. But this one was born with thirteen deformities, one for each curse her mother had sworn. This child Kiel cursed the most because the infant was so ugly and deformed. The baby had one leg shorter than the other, one arm bent the wrong way, an ear set at an awkward place. Kiel even cursed her daughter with the name Shaetore, which means 'she who brings death.' Because Shaetore was so deformed, she made it impossible for Kiel to

43

have any more children. In those days it was considered a great tragedy—equivalent to death—for a princess not to give birth to a suitable heir."

"She must have been one ugly baby," Sally said.

Ann Templeton scowled at her. "She was her mother's daughter. It was not her fault she was born deformed. Her mother should have loved her as she would any child. But Kiel thought only of herself, of her position in the kingdom. She felt that fate had made a fool of her. In her bitterness, she sent her brother to abandon Shaetore in the woods. Just to leave the child out among the trees and let the animals eat the poor girl. Kiel's brother, Harome, took to the task with a heavy heart. He did agree to it, though, because he was afraid to disobey his powerful sister. As he carried the baby deep into the woods, he kept staring into her eyes. There was hardly a spot on Shaetore's body that didn't suffer from deformity, but her deep blue eyes were remarkably clear and shiny. The more Harome stared into them, the more convinced he became that he could not abandon this child. Yet what could he do? He knew Kiel was insane with bitterness. If he did not carry out her order he himself would be killed.

"Eventually he came to a clearing where a solitary tree stump stood in the center. It was a wide stump, polished smooth, and was waist high. Harome thought it a decent place to leave the baby—as decent as any he could find in the woods. Still he knew he was committing a great sin by abandoning the child. He knew she could not last long in the wild, a night at most. It was with a breaking heart that he turned away from the infant and began to walk back toward the kingdom.

"Then something miraculous happened. With each step he took away from the child, he acquired one of the child's deformities. With one step his right leg shortened. With the next his back grew a hump on it. With the third he developed a huge boil on his right cheek. By the time he reached the edge of the clearing, he was a grown-up version of Shaetore. Of course he knew it was a sign that he had to overcome his fear of Kiel and save the child.

"As Harome stepped back toward the baby his deformities began to fall away. When he finally held Shaetore in his hands again, he was completely normal. Unfortunately the child was still deformed, and he didn't know what to do with her. He had no supplies, no money. He didn't know whom he could turn to for help.

"At that time there lived in the woods a powerful wizard named Zy. Zy was very old and by the alchemy of his magical arts was capable of living still longer. He was also well aware of Kiel's curses and Shaetore's deformities. From the time Harome had entered the woods carrying the baby, Zy had been following them. He had not planned to save the child. Zy was the type of wizard who tried not to interfere in other people's business. But as Harome picked up the baby and looked around the woods, he let out a cry begging anyone to tell him what to do next. Zy, who was watching from the trees and who identified with the entire universe, decided that was his cue to step forward and introduce himself.

"Harome was delighted to meet Zy and begged him to take the child and raise her. Zy was not anxious to become a single parent at such an advanced age, but, like Harome, when he stared into the child's eyes he felt their strange magic. He took the baby on the condition that when Shaetore was old enough, she would be allowed to return to the kingdom and take her rightful place as a princess of the realm. To this Harome readily agreed, although he didn't exactly know how that would be possible. You understand of course that Harome was just happy to be rid of the child, without guilt. He decided that he would worry about Shaetore's return to the kingdom later.

"Zy took Shaetore back to his cave and set about the task of raising her, which was not easy given her many deformities. Shaetore was sick half the time because her deformities extended even to her internal organs. She couldn't even digest the goat's milk that Zy fed her. He had to develop exotic herbal potions just to keep her alive. Indeed, Shaetore lived on Zy's herbal teas, and nothing else, for the first ten years of her life.

"In all this time, as she grew, she would ask about where she came from. Who her parents were and why she could not see them. To these questions Zy tried to give the best answers that he could invent, but Shaetore was too shrewd for him, even at such a young age. Eventually she forced the truth out of him, and that was a hard day for both of them. Shaetore sank into a deep depression and went off into the woods for days at a time. Zy didn't know what to do and regretted that he had said anything to her. But if the truth be known, he could not have resisted the power of Shaetore's gaze. Great wizard that he was, he was no match for her. Shaetore had been born under the spell of thirteen curses aimed at the universe. Thirteen was and still is an evil number. Later some wise men said that Shaetore was born as an instrument of the universe's revenge. I don't know if that is true, but it is a disturbing theory.

"Shaetore continued to grow, in power but unfortunately not in beauty. Her deformities just grew with her and made her difficult to look upon. During these years she began to learn Zy's craft, his knowledge of herbs and spells and alchemy. Not only did Shaetore learn everything the wizard knew, she expanded upon his knowledge. Shaetore had been born with that rarest of gifts—true intuition. As she wandered in the forest at night information came to her. Even as she stared up at the moon, great secrets would be revealed to her. For even then Shaetore preferred the darkness over the light. Perhaps it was something deep and dark in her heart. Perhaps already she was thinking of the revenge she would take on her mother, the famous Princess Kiel, queen of all Atlantis. Even deep in the woods, Shaetore had heard of her mother's rise to power.

"Precisely how Shaetore changed herself into a vampire is unclear. All we know is that the transformation was triggered by a human sacrifice. One night when Zy was sitting under his favorite tree smoking a pipe, Shaetore suddenly returned with Harome in tow. Or I should say in chains because he was her prisoner. Without Zy's knowledge,

Shaetore had traveled to the kingdom and abducted Harome. Even though Zy had explained to Shaetore the circumstances under which Harome had turned her over to him, she obviously blamed her uncle and wanted to take her revenge on him by using his blood as the secret and most evil ingredient in a formula to give her perfect health and incredible beauty. Even I cannot imagine what was in that formula. I only know that Shaetore somehow called down the energies of the full moon and infused that power into Harome's blood as it dripped into her mouth. Shaetore did not just take a few drops from Harome. She drained him until he was a corpse."

"Did Zy observe this transformation?" Watch interrupted.

"Yes," Ann Templeton said.

"Why didn't he stop her?" Adam asked. "You said he was a good wizard. He knew what she was doing was evil."

Ann Templeton's expression was sad. "He didn't stop her because he loved her. She had told him that this was the only way she could be beautiful, and he believed her. And she was right, she did become beautiful. But when it was over Harome was dead, and Shaetore could show her beauty only during the night. In fact, she couldn't bear the sun

CHRISTOPHER PIKE

anymore. And to maintain her beauty she had to have blood every night. But other changes had come upon her as well, perhaps changes even she had not foreseen. She was extremely powerful, physically as well as mentally, and she never aged. Not only that, she could make more of her kind by drinking and sharing her blood with ordinary people."

"What did Zy think of all this?" Watch asked.

"His opinion was not asked for," Ann Templeton said. "Zy was the first person Shaetore changed into a vampire. She forced him to become one. He is still with her to this day, I believe."

"Is he evil?" Adam asked.

The witch shrugged. "He's a fifty-thousand-year-old vampire. But perhaps he remembers his beginnings and how he didn't choose to become what he is. He might not be all evil."

"Did Shaetore return to the kingdom and take revenge upon her mother?" Watch asked.

"Yes," Ann Templeton said. "She returned with great numbers of vampires and transformed her mother into a vampire and made her her servant. But she could not overcome the army of her father, Prince Rankte. She and her kind were driven from the kingdom. Most were slain, but a few survived and so the legends of vampires survive to this day."

"Why would Shaetore come here?" Adam asked. "Why now?"

"She is drawn to places of power—she always has been," Ann Templeton said. "Whatever you think of Spooksville, there is tremendous energy here. If she intends to start another army of vampires, she probably thinks this is as good a place as any."

"But how can she be stopped?" Adam asked.

"She can be stopped only if a wooden stake is driven through her heart," the witch said.

"We know that already," Sally complained.

"She must have some other vulnerable spot?" Watch asked.

"Not that I know of," the witch said.

"But what about your powers?" Adam said. "Can't you stop her?"

Ann Templeton spoke with heavy reluctance. "I don't know for sure. But I do know that if I were to face Shaetore directly, I would have to call forth such power that all of Spooksville would be laid waste in the process."

"But you haven't told us anything that could help us defeat her," Sally said.

"I never said I would," the witch told her. "You asked about her origins. I have told you. I cannot help you in your fight against her, at least not directly. I have told you before, you must carry out your own battles."

"What are you going to do, then?" Sally asked bitterly. "Stay here and fortify your castle against a vampire attack? The whole town could be vampires by tomorrow night."

The witch stared at her. "That is exactly what I am going to do. I told you, if I face Shaetore myself, none of you will survive."

Watch stood. "I appreciate your help, Ms. Templeton. You have given us great insight into the psychology of our enemy. We will use that insight, and we will find a way to destroy her."

Adam also stood. "I feel better knowing who she is. I just hope we can destroy her."

Ann Templeton slowly got to her feet, signaling that their meeting was over. As she stared at them, a faint smile touched her lips. But it didn't last. It seemed as if, for once, she was not sure if she would see them again.

"Shaetore has destroyed thousands," she said. "She will try to anticipate your every move. But know that she cannot read your minds. That she must have weak spots, even if I don't know what they are." She paused and nodded her head. "I wish you all luck. You will need it."

5

Cindy Makey had lied to her friends. Lied to them because she was too softhearted and couldn't stop worrying about Ted Tane. Rather than heading straight home, Cindy walked straight to the hospital.

But she wasn't allowed in to see her classmate until after sunset. The nurse from the night before, Sharon RN, led her into Ted's room.

"Don't stay long," the nurse warned. "He's not fully recovered."

"But he is better than he was this morning?" Cindy asked anxiously.

The nurse smiled—she had a nice smile. "Yes. He's getting better all the time."

"That's good," Cindy said, thinking that if he was getting better—in the nurse's opinion—then he couldn't be a vampire. She opened the door and stepped into the room.

Ted was sitting up and reading a book, an act that also had the effect of relaxing her. Cindy couldn't imagine that a vampire would ever stop to read. Of course Cindy didn't stop to think that a vampire might be full of all kinds of tricks.

The room was uncomfortably cold.

She figured the heating must be broken.

Ted looked over and smiled at her.

He had a lovely smile. Lovely white teeth.

He set his book aside and waved her over.

"Hello," he said. "I'm glad you came back."

Cindy approached the bed. "How are you doing? Are you feeling better?"

"Much better."

"You still look kind of pale."

Ted shrugged. "I was in critical condition. It will take me time to recover." He gestured to a spot on the bed beside him. "Would you like to sit down, Cindy?"

"Yes, thank you." She sat on the bed not far from him. He stared at her with his bright eyes. They were still slightly bloodshot but definitely clearer. She found herself taken by them; actually she found it hard not to stare into them. Ted seemed to take pleasure in her scrutiny.

"What did you do today?" he asked.

"What?" she asked, blinking.

"You and your friends. What did you do after you left here this morning?"

She blushed. She felt embarrassed about what they had done even though, all of a sudden, she couldn't remember the visit to the warehouse clearly. She wondered why that was.

"I don't know," she said evasively. "We just hung out."

He spoke to her in a soft but powerful voice.

"You didn't do anything special?" he asked.

"No."

"You didn't go anywhere special?"

"No," she said.

He leaned closer. His eyes grew larger.

"Are you sure, Cindy?" he asked.

She stammered. "Well, we did go out to the old warehouse on Trumbell. That's at the edge of town, you know."

"What did you do out there?" he asked.

She didn't want to tell him. Just the thought of the fire they had started disturbed her. Yet she didn't want to lie to him, either. It seemed, when she wasn't straight with him, that his eyes hurt her slightly. She was sure she was imagining it, but the impression was there nevertheless. She tried glancing away, but that hurt as well and she returned to staring into his eyes. He had such deep eyes—she never really noticed them before.

"Nothing," she said.

He leaned even closer. As he did so, he opened his mouth a little more and she saw his teeth a little clearer. He seemed to have more teeth than most boys his age. More teeth than most humans.

"Tell me about this nothing," he said.

There was an edge to his voice, and the words came out like an order.

"We went inside the warehouse," she said, and her voice sounded drugged to her own ears.

"What did you do inside the warehouse?"

"We looked around," she said.

"What did you look for?"

"Why do you want to—"

"Tell me," he interrupted before she could finish.

Cindy found she was struggling for breath. For that matter, she could hardly move. It was as if her body as well as her will had turned to stone. She felt as if she must answer his questions truthfully, that there was no other choice.

"We looked for vampires," she heard herself say.

Ted's smile widened. "Did you find any?"

"Yes."

"How many?"

"I don't know. We found one. But . . ."

"But what?" he demanded.

"We think there might have been more there."

"And what did you do with this vampire you found?"

Cindy hesitated. She didn't want to answer that question. She feared if she did, Ted would get mad. And she was suddenly afraid to make him mad. Still, she couldn't resist his eyes. It was as if they were twin knives drilling into her brain. Cold knives that froze her thoughts in place.

"We torched the vampire," Cindy answered.

Ted lost his smile. "Why did you do that?"

Cindy struggled for an answer. It seemed as if there were no logical reason for what they had done. Yet a part of her knew there must be one. Only around Ted, sitting so close to his swelling eyes, it seemed as if logic itself did not exist.

"Because he was a monster," she said, fighting to get the words out. "Because if we didn't destroy him he would make others of his kind and destroy the whole town."

The sentences, the explanation, fairly exhausted her.

She literally could not catch her breath.

Ted sat back and kept staring at her.

"Do you know what I am?" he asked.

She shook her head slightly.

His smile crept back, like a lizard across his mouth.

"I am a monster, Cindy," he said.

She swallowed thickly. "No."

"Yes, it's true. You're alone in this hospital room with a monster." He glanced toward the covered window. No light was coming in from outside. All of a sudden it seemed to Cindy as though there was no light in the room, even though the corner lamp was still on. He added in a cocky tone, "You're alone with a vampire after dark. Do you know what that means?"

Cindy shook her head. "You can't be a vampire."

His lizard grin grew. "Why not?"

"Because you're my friend. I'm your friend. I came here as a friend."

He leaned close once more. "That was your mistake, Cindy. Vampires have no friends. They have only servants or victims. Which do you want to be?"

She continued to have trouble speaking. Her fear was growing at astronomical speed. A part of her knew she was in extreme danger. Another part was trying to get her body off the bed and out the door. The only problem was that all these parts were not communicating. It was because of his eyes, she realized. They had her hypnotized. She could see the evil in them now. It was as clear as the blood in them.

Cindy wondered if he had had blood before she arrived.

Dinner. She wondered if he was still thirsty.

"I don't want to be either," she whispered. "I just want to go home."

He shook his head in mock sorrow.

"I'm afraid it is much too late for that. After tonight you will never return home. At least not to a home you recognize. Did you know that it was in my own home that my parents attacked me and changed me into what I am now? I tried to escape, but not before they did their work on me. That is why you haven't been able to get hold of them today. They've been sleeping in the basement."

Cindy tried to get off the bed and stand.

Ted grabbed her by the wrists. He was very strong.

"Let me go," she moaned.

"I can't."

"Please," she begged. "I won't hurt you."

He grinned. He thought she was funny.

"But I'm going to hurt you," he said. "But before I do, you have to answer my question. What do you want to be?"

Tears streamed over Cindy's face. "I don't understand."

Ted's mouth was now as big as his eyes. It was as if he were ready to swallow her alive. He moved closer still, and she could feel his cold breath on her trembling face.

"Do you want me to feed off you?" he asked. "To drain you of blood and let you die here in this room? That could be a mercy. When you are dead all feeling ends, good and bad. Or do you want me to give you some of my blood as well? To turn you into a vampire?"

Cindy closed her eyes and wept.

Still the spell of his eyes, the grip of his hands, did not end.

"I don't want you to do anything to me," she cried.

She heard Ted laugh. It was more of a wild beast's cackle. She felt his mouth draw closer still, his sharp nails reach up to her neck.

"You are too precious to kill," he whispered in her ear. "I think I will make you immortal."

Cindy felt his sharp teeth brush her soft skin.

She felt a deep and penetrating pain.

There was the metallic smell of blood.

Then she found herself sinking into blackness.

6

The gang had hardly left the witch's castle when they were attacked by three vampires. They recognized none of them. Once again, they must have been old vampires Shaetore had brought with her to Spooksville. Two female and one male—they were all dressed in black, and their red eyes glowed in the dark. They had obviously been waiting outside the castle, waiting to destroy them.

"Light your flares!" Watch ordered. "Form a defensive circle. Don't let them come up behind you. Let's try to hold them off."

"Let's get back to the castle!" Bryce said as he struck his flares to life.

"We can't," Adam answered, glancing over his

shoulder. "The witch has already raised her draw-bridge. We have to fight them alone."

"She sent us out here to die," Sally complained.

"We're not going to die," Watch said, holding out his burning flares.

Yet for the moment they weren't sure what to do. The vampires had circled them but had backed off a distance of fifty feet. Clearly the fire disturbed them, but they seemed to know it would eventually burn out. The vampires could move with deftness and speed. The gang had to shift position so quickly to keep them at bay that they started to get dizzy. The red glow of the vampires' eyes was disturbing. It was almost as if the monsters were willing them to set their torches down. Adam had to fight against the impulse.

"Don't look into their eyes," he warned the others. "They're trying to hypnotize us."

"I feel it," Sally said weakly.

"We have to get out of here and seek shelter," Watch said.

"Wherever we go we'll just get trapped," Bryce said grimly. "We can't outrun them. I say we lower our torches and invite their attack. Maybe we can get stakes into their chests."

"We can't beat them by force," Watch said. "We

have to trick them somehow. Let's move in the direction of the school."

"What's there?" Sally demanded.

"The gymnasium," Watch said.

"What's in there?" Adam asked.

"Hope," Watch said.

In a shifting circle of sparks they moved toward the school. The vampires gave them a larger berth. They were clearly waiting for the torches to go out to make their move. But because the gang still had to hold the monsters back, it took them close to half an hour to reach the gym. By then their torches were almost exhausted.

The gymnasium was locked, but they had no trouble forcing the door open—not with three vampires breathing down their necks. Fear gave them added strength. The moment they were inside they bound the door with a piece of chain. Bryce spoke for all of them.

"If we can break in here, they can break in here," Bryce said. "This door won't hold them. Why are we here? We've just trapped ourselves."

"No," Watch said. "I have an idea. Let's hang our flares underneath the bleachers and try to hide near the gym entrance."

"Are you crazy?" Sally asked. "Our flares are the

only things holding them off. Without them they'll be on us in a minute."

"Our flares are going out in a few minutes anyway," Watch said. "When the vampires do break in here, they'll be momentarily confused about our location. They'll rush toward the flares. Then we'll have a chance to escape."

"To run away?" Bryce asked doubtfully. "I don't think so. They'll be on us in seconds."

"Just trust me," Watch said.

"I'll trust you," Adam said. "I don't know what else to do."

They hurried under the bleachers. They could hear the three vampires pounding at the door. They could tell the door wouldn't hold for long. Quickly, under Watch's direction, they jammed what was left of their flares into the metal bars that held up the bleachers. Then they raced for the closest entrance and hid.

The vampires broke through the door.

They raced toward the flares under the bleachers.

Watch leaped up and reached for a nearby button.

The bleachers began to fold up.

"Of course!" Bryce cried. "The bleachers fold up when we need extra space in here."

The bleachers continued to collapse on the vampires. They had been caught by surprise and didn't understand the danger they were in—and that they had been tricked—until it was too late. They tried to escape onto the gym floor, but by then the bleachers had collapsed too far. There was nothing for the monsters to do as the powerful bleacher motors drove the stands against the wall.

The gang didn't hang around to see the end of their enemy. They raced out into the fresh air through the door the vampires had broken in. They were relieved to see no more vampires.

"What are we going to do now?" Bryce asked as they ran out of the school grounds. "I don't think we're going to get away with that trick again."

"We cannot try to defeat each vampire we come to," Watch said. "We have to go for Queen Shaetore and destroy her. That's our only hope."

"But nothing the witch said gave us a clue to where she could be," Adam said.

"She did give us one clue," Watch said. "She said the queen would be where we least expected."

"She also said the queen would want revenge for what we did this afternoon," Adam said. "I think this attack confirms that. I want to get to Cindy before we do anything else. Shaetore might have sent someone after her already."

"I agree," Watch said.

Cindy was not at home, and her mother said she hadn't seen her all day. In panic the group gathered outside her house.

"The queen might have got her already," Sally said.

"I'm not so sure," Adam said, thinking. "According to Cindy's mother, she never came home, even though she promised she would. But Cindy is a person who keeps her word. The only reason she would have lied was because she intended to do something we wouldn't have approved of."

"You're right," Watch said. "She must have gone to see Ted."

"That slimy vampire?" Sally asked. "Why?"

"Because she believed he could be saved," Adam said. "We shouldn't have been threatening his life every few minutes."

"I never threatened his life," Sally said. Then she added, "Well, maybe once or twice. But he is a vampire, you know. We should have cut out his heart when we had the chance."

"What we should have done doesn't matter," Watch said. "We have to get to the hospital before it's too late."

"It's probably too late already," Bryce warned.

Once again they found the hospital strangely

deserted. This time there wasn't even a nurse on duty at the front desk. They didn't let it slow them down. As a group they rushed down the hallways to Ted's room. They were so scared about what might have happened to Cindy that they practically kicked open his hospital door.

Ted's bed was empty.

Ted had already checked out.

Perhaps for the next few thousand years.

But Cindy was in the room. Oh, yes.

She was sitting on the floor in a corner.

Sitting in a pool of blood and staring with unfocused eyes.

She moaned softly, and there was red on her lips.

"Hi," she said in a thick voice.

7

They were by her side in seconds. No, that wasn't exactly true. Adam and Watch hurried to be with Cindy. But Bryce and Sally kept a respectful distance. They both were still carrying wooden stakes in their belts. And from the look in their eyes, it didn't appear as if they were beyond using them on their friend.

"Cindy!" Adam said with grief. "What happened to you?"

She kept her head bowed slightly but managed to stare at him. There were red veins in the whites of her eyes. Yet Adam wasn't sure if she really saw him. Or if she still recognized him as a friend.

"Don't know," she mumbled.

"Was Ted here?" Watch asked. "Did he do anything to you?"

Her eyes rolled lazily in Watch's direction.

She didn't seem to recognize him, either.

"Ted," she muttered, her head still down. "No Ted."

Watch reached for her chin to raise her head.

There were bloody teeth marks on her neck.

"She's a vampire!" Sally gasped.

"We have to destroy her," Bryce said.

"We're not destroying Cindy!" Adam snapped at him, and there was pain in his voice. "She has been hurt. We have to help her."

Bryce moved closer, his hand on one of the stakes.

"She has not simply been hurt," Bryce said. "Ted has transformed her into a vampire. If we don't destroy her now, she will attack us."

Watch glanced up at him. "She may have vampiric blood in her veins, but she is still in the period of transformation. We might be able to reverse the process—there's hope."

"There's no hope," Bryce said, and his voice trembled with pain. He was obviously struggling to get the words out. He loved Cindy as much as any of them. "We have to face reality. She is one of them. To kill her now would be a kindness."

Sally stepped forward. "No. We can't kill her."

Bryce turned to her. "You know what has happened here. We can't unmake what has been done."

There were tears in Sally's eyes, perhaps in all their eyes.

"And we can't just destroy her," Sally said. "I know it's a foolish and hopeless risk, but we have to try to do something." She reached out and touched Bryce's hand, the one that held the wooden stake. Sally added, "We owe her that much."

Bryce lowered his head and nodded weakly.

"I just don't know what can be done," he whispered. "All the legends say that once the blood of a vampire has been put into one's system, it cannot be removed."

Adam stared at Cindy through teary eyes. Her gaze seemed to be wandering all over the room, unable to focus on anyone or anything in particular. Adam brushed her cheek and marveled at the chill of her skin. The entire room seemed to be caught in an arctic zone.

"She's so white," he muttered.

Watch nodded. "Ted must have drained her of blood before he gave her an infusion of his own blood." He paused and closed his eyes as if deep in thought. Then he reopened them and stared at Cindy. "I wonder if a transfusion of normal human blood could slow down the transformation process."

Adam jumped at the idea. "You're a genius, Watch. We're in a hospital. We should be able to get plenty of blood. Let's try to find a doctor."

Watch held up his hand. "The transfusion idea is at best a temporary measure. We still have to get to Queen Shaetore to end this madness. And I'm thinking we might be able to use Cindy to find her."

Bryce and Sally knelt beside them. It didn't appear as if Cindy was going to attack them soon.

"How can we do that?" Sally asked.

Watch gestured at Cindy. "Look at her. She's in some kind of trance—almost as if she were hypnotized. I wonder if it's possible that the queen is slowly casting a spell over her mind, from a distance. From Ann Templeton's account I got the impression that all the vampires were under Shaetore's control."

"That's true," Adam said. "She's their boss."

"But how can that help us?" Bryce asked. "It sounds like that might make us even more vulnerable. Shaetore might already know that we're here."

"We might be able to use Cindy's trance state in reverse," Watch explained. "To get her to tell us where Shaetore is right now."

"But how?" Sally asked.

"Let's see," Watch said, turning his attention back to Cindy. "Cindy, close your eyes."

Cindy stared at him for a moment, then closed her eyes.

"She does appear sensitive to suggestion," Adam whispered.

Watch nodded. "This connection might be the break we've been looking for." He leaned close to Cindy and spoke in her ear. "Cindy, I want you to describe what you see. Don't think about it, just talk."

Cindy replied slowly, as if someone else were using her vocal cords.

"I see red," she said.

"Is red all you see?" Watch asked.

"I see red," Cindy mumbled with her eyes still shut.

"What else do you see?"

"Cold."

"How can you see cold?" Sally wanted to know.

"Shh," Watch cautioned. "Are you in a cold place?"

"Yes."

"Where is this place?"

"I don't know."

"Why are you there?" Watch asked.

"The blood."

"There is blood in this place?"

"Yes."

"Whose blood is it?"

"I don't know."

"Are there human bodies in this place?"

"No."

"Is this a large place?"

"No."

"Is it a room?"

"Yes."

"And this place is filled with blood?"

"Yes."

"Is the blood in plastic bags or bottles?"

"Yes."

"Is this place near where we are now?"

"Yes."

"Is Queen Shaetore in this place?"

At this question Cindy's eyes popped open and a red light shone deep inside them. Her voice grew thick and cold with threats as she glared at Watch.

"You will not be told!" she shouted.

Watch met her burning gaze and did not flinch.

"Close your eyes, Cindy, and rest," he said gently.

As Cindy relaxed, the others turned to Watch for answers.

"Did Shaetore speak through her?" Bryce asked.

"At the end, yes," Watch said, "but at first Cindy was merely seeing through Shaetore's eyes."

"It's too bad she was interrupted," Sally said. "I think she was just about to tell us where the queen is."

Watch glanced fondly at Cindy. Their poor friend was breathing in short, rapid gasps. It was almost as if she could no longer draw oxygen from the air. Watch had to stop and wipe at his eyes. But he managed to keep his voice steady as he replied to Sally.

"Cindy told us enough," he said. "I know where Shaetore is."

"Where?" they asked all at once.

"In this hospital," Watch said.

"What?" they gasped.

"Adam, you said it yourself a moment ago," Watch replied. "We're in a hospital, and hospitals keep large supplies of blood on hand. What better place for thirsty Shaetore to hang out? Also notice Cindy's description of the place she was seeing. A cold enclosed room with blood in bags and bottles, but where there are no bodies. Finally notice how cold it is in here. Ted, as he changed into a vampire, must have wanted it that way. That must mean vampires prefer cold to warmth. What better place for the queen of all the vampires to hang out than a cold locker where blood is stored?" Watch nodded. "She's in this hospital, I'm sure of it."

Bryce pulled a stake from his belt. "Then let's get her."

"Not so fast," Watch said. "I want to check out the rest of the hospital."

"What for?" Adam asked.

Watch squeezed Cindy's arm.

"An unexpected weapon," he said.

8

But when Watch left Ted's hospital room in the company of Adam, he didn't search for a weapon at all. What he did do was break into a drug locker and paw through all kinds of medicines and needles. Adam stared at him in confusion.

"You're not going to get a chance to give her a shot," Adam said.

"There are shots and there are shots," Watch said.

"What does that mean?"

"I hope you get a chance to see."

They returned to Ted's room, where the others were waiting.

Cindy was still staring in a daze.

But she had begun to lick the red stuff on her lips.

Ted's blood, they knew. It was hard to look at her.

A decision had to be made about Cindy. Sally and Bryce wanted to leave her in the hospital room while they went after the queen. Adam was against the idea.

"We don't know if she'll be here when we get back," Adam said.

"But she's safer here than with us," Bryce said.

"You're saying that you don't trust her," Adam snapped back.

"No," Bryce said.

"That's exactly what he's saying, and I have to agree with him," Sally said. "Look at her, Adam, we can't trust her in this condition. Any minute now she's going to want to take a bite out of our necks."

Adam shook his head. "Cindy won't hurt us. It's not possible. Watch, you tell them."

"Tell them what?" Watch asked, his pockets stuffed with drugs and needles. "They're probably right."

Adam was hurt. "But if we leave her alone here, she might get up and wander out of the hospital.

We can't let that happen. We might never find her again." He briefly closed his eyes at the agony of the thought. "We might never see her again."

"You're really afraid that she might leave here to go feed," Bryce said. "That urge will sweep over her soon enough."

It seemed the decision was left up to Watch. He struggled over the choices for more than a minute. The pressure he felt, as he stared at Cindy, was what the others were feeling. Watch finally shook his head.

"We'll take her with us," he said. "She belongs with us, for good or evil."

"I think you just made the worst decision of your life, Watch," Sally said.

Yet they felt too pressured for time to argue further. Helping Cindy to her feet, they led her out of Ted's room and into the hospital hallway. They had no idea where the freezer was that held the blood, but it didn't take them long to find it. They weren't surprised to find the door shut.

"Maybe she's left already," Sally whispered outside the door.

"I don't think so," Adam muttered, keeping Cindy upright. Her gaze was going more and more often to his neck. She had even run her hand through his hair on occasion. He pretended to ignore her, but she was making him nervous. Adam added, "There's something evil in there, I feel it."

"She's in there," Watch said, puzzled. "But I'm surprised she waited for us. She must have figured out how we used Cindy to locate her."

"Then we're walking into a trap," Sally said. "She just wants to turn us all into vampires."

"That would be a great victory for her," Bryce said grimly. "We're probably the only people on earth capable of stopping her from achieving world conquest."

"We have no choice," Adam said. "We have to face her now because we may never get another chance."

"I agree," Watch said. "Is everyone ready?"

"I have my stakes and one flare left," Sally said. "How can I defeat the queen of all vampires with that?"

"We need faith more than powerful weapons," Watch said.

"We need blind luck," Bryce muttered.

They stepped toward the freezer door.

Bryce unlatched it. The door swung open.

Shadows waited for them inside. And cold.

And a voice. A soft and gentle voice they all recognized.

"Welcome," it said.

Watch shone a flashlight beam into the interior of the freezer.

Amidst the frost and blood stood Queen Shae-tore.

The enemy of all who walked and breathed beneath the sun.

The original vampire. Fifty thousand years old.

Yet they recognized her. They knew her.

"Nurse Sharon," Watch said quietly. "I should have guessed."

She smiled at them, her sweet smile.

Yet they could see her fangs, barely hidden beneath her red lips.

"Please come in," she said. "I've been waiting for you."

9

They slowly entered the giant cooler. Bryce held a stake ready, Sally a flare. Watch carried a needle filled with clear fluid—in his pocket—and Adam supported Cindy. They were ready to do battle, yet Shaetore seemed at ease. In her clean white nurse's uniform with the friendly name badge, she didn't appear threatening. Yet there was something dark in her wide eyes. It was hard to think that at one time she had been deformed. She was so beautiful now.

Plastic bags of red blood hung all around.

Many had been torn apart. And drained.

"How are my heroes?" she asked as they drew close.

"We're not your heroes," Sally snapped.

Shaetore smiled. "But you are heroes neverthe-less. I have heard stories of you. You drive off monsters and aliens, witches and ghosts. I have looked forward to meeting you in battle, to see what you will do to me."

Bryce fingered his wooden stake.

"We will destroy you," he said proudly.

Shaetore mocked him. "Do you think you can? I am very old, you know. I am sure your witch told you that. I am not so easy to destroy."

"You know Ann Templeton?" Adam asked.

"Of course. I have dealt with several of her ancestors in the past. She did not tell you? None of them survived our encounters. At least not as witches."

"You changed them into vampires?" Watch asked.

"Yes." Shaetore added casually, "As I will change you."

"We're not so easy to destroy, either," Adam said defiantly.

Shaetore turned her attention to him. "You don't need to hold her up, Adam. She's growing stronger by the second."

Adam let go of Cindy and stepped to the side. Cindy seemed transfixed by Shaetore, which worried Adam. But he didn't have time to help his friend, not at the moment. He kept his attention focused on Shaetore.

"Why are you here in Spooksville?" he demanded.

Shaetore shrugged. "My intentions must be obvious."

"Why have you waited so long to start a new wave of vampires?" Watch asked.

Shaetore momentarily lost her casual air. She seemed to absorb the question and then reflect upon it with all the knowledge and experience of her ancient memory.

"I come at this time because humanity is sick," she said finally. "The material world is all that matters to them. They have forgotten the magic of the elements, the secret powers of nature. It is my purpose to remove that disease."

"By turning everyone into a vampire?" Adam asked. "Pardon me, but that seems like a stupid plan."

Shaetore threw her head back and laughed. "You'd have to live for ten thousand years to begin to understand my plans." She lowered her voice. "Even now you don't understand how you came to be here."

With those words Shaetore nodded slightly.

Suddenly the room darkened.

Cindy had shut the door behind them.

They had only the beam from Watch's flashlight to see by. Sally quickly lit a flare. The sparks smoked in the chilly air. Adam whirled on Cindy.

"Cindy! You don't have to listen to her," he said.

"But she does have to listen," Shaetore corrected. "She belongs to me now. Soon you will as well, and I will send you out into the wide world to wipe out all of humanity."

Sally took a step forward, holding the flare out.

"That's not going to happen, Queen Bloodsucker," she threatened.

Shaetore smiled. "Only my younger children are intimidated by fire. There isn't a weapon you know of that can destroy me."

"I wouldn't be so sure of that," Bryce said dangerously.

Shaetore eyed his stake. Then she spread her arms wide.

"Come, young hero," she said. "Destroy the evil monster."

Bryce took the invitation seriously. He slashed forward with his stake, aimed directly at her chest. But in a motion their eyes could not follow, Shaetore caught his stake and broke it in half. Then she casually offered it back to him.

"Do you have anything more potent in your bag of tricks?" she asked.

In a rage Sally threw her flare at Shaetore.

The ancient queen caught it by the fiery end and slowly put the flames out in her open palm. She didn't even grimace in pain; the fire had absolutely no effect upon her flesh. The freezer filled with bitter smoke. Shaetore slowly turned to Watch.

"You are known in certain circles for your profound insights," she said. "More than all the others, I have waited to face you. But it seems you have brought no weapon to destroy me. Why is that, Watch?"

Watch sighed as he stared into her face.

"Because I realized earlier, when the witch spoke of you, that we could never defeat you by force," he said.

Shaetore seemed pleased. "Then you surrender to me?"

Watch slowly nodded. "If you will make me immortal."

"Watch," Sally said, outraged. "You don't want to be a bloodsucker for the next ten thousand years. Do something. Don't give up without a fight!"

"We can't fight her," Watch said, seeming to fall under the spell of Shaetore. The queen of the vampires held out her hand.

"Come to me," she said. "You will go first."

Watch stepped toward her. He moved as if drugged, staggering slightly. They all thought he was under her control.

"Watch!" Adam cried.

Yet it was too late. Already Watch stood before the evil queen.

"Raise your chin," Shaetore said, as she leaned toward him and bared her fangs. "Turn your head to the side. There will be pain for only a moment, then you will know a sweetness unimaginable."

Watch clearly could not resist.

He swayed where he stood.

Queen Shaetore bent closer.

Her teeth were inches from the flesh of his throat.

"Watch!" Sally screamed.

It was then Watch struck.

From out of his pocket he whipped a syringe filled with drugs. It was a bold move on his part and obviously a calculated one. Unfortunately his best reflexes must have appeared to be in slow motion to Shaetore. She laughed as she intercepted his needle and cracked it in her hand. The liquid drugs dripped onto the floor.

"I expected something like that," she said, showing all her teeth, literally gloating over Watch, who was now in her grip. "Good try, Watch, but you were right the first time. You were defeated before you even began to fight me. I am too old, too wise, too powerful. And right now I am very thirsty."

Shaetore picked Watch off his feet and pressed her mouth into his neck.

They heard the sound of her teeth slipping deep into his flesh.

They saw Watch's blood swell around the vampire's lips.

And they found they could not move.

She had power over them all.

They could only stare in horror as she drank his blood.

"Watch," Sally wept pitifully.

It was over—they knew it was finally over.

Then something very strange happened.

Shaetore suddenly let go of Watch and staggered back.

Her dark eyes flared with a red light, then dimmed.

Watch also staggered away from her.

It was as if both of them were having trouble standing.

"What have you done?" Shaetore screamed at Watch as his blood dripped from her lips. She leaned against the rear of the cubicle for support.

All her great power seemed to waver. But even though Watch was on the verge of collapse, he managed a faint smile.

"I gave myself a shot as I walked in here," he said. "Now that drug is putting us both to sleep." Moving in slow motion, Watch turned to the others. "There's not much time," he whispered.

Then he collapsed in their arms.

Shaetore was also sliding onto the floor.

Yet her eyes remained open. She was still scary.

"Try to take me now," she mocked them in a weak voice. "It will be your death."

They believed her.

Grabbing Watch and Cindy, they fled from the freezer.

They didn't stop running until they were far from the hospital.

10

Eventually they had to stop. They were still herding Cindy around, and Watch they were actually carrying. He was sound asleep, snoring peacefully. His neck bled slightly, and they wondered if he would turn into a vampire next. They set him down on the sidewalk on his back while they tried to figure out what to do next.

"We shouldn't have run," Sally chided herself and the others. "Watch gave us a good shot at her. With those drugs in her system she was vulnerable. We should have attacked her right then and given it all we had."

"I think she would have beaten us still," Bryce said.

"It doesn't matter what we should have done," Adam said. "What we do now is all that matters."

Bryce nodded grimly in Cindy's direction. She stood leaning against a lamp post, staring off into the distance. Yet with each passing minute she seemed less helpless.

"We have to get away from Cindy," Bryce said. "Shaetore will know where to find us through her. Remember, the connection between them runs both ways."

"I agree," Sally said reluctantly. "We can't even talk about our next move with her with us." Sally paused. "Plus she could attack us any second. In fact, she'll probably attack me first. You know we've never really gotten along."

Adam shook his head. "We are not leaving her out here in the dark."

"I bet she likes the dark by now," Sally muttered.

Adam was adamant. "No. We stay together."

"That sounds so noble and brave," Bryce said with an edge to his voice. "But it is also impractical. How do we keep her from changing into a vampire? If you can answer me that, then we can keep her with us."

Adam considered. "We talked about this at the hospital. We can give her transfusions of normal human blood."

"The only place we can get blood is back at the hospital," Sally said. "Back at Madame Shaetore's freezer. And I don't think she'll offer us any."

"That's not the only place where there is blood," Adam said. He pulled a couple of needles, plastic tubing, and a small glass bottle out of his pocket. "While Watch was going through the medicine cabinet, I grabbed this stuff."

"What for?" Sally asked.

Adam glanced at Cindy. "I am going to give her my blood," he said.

"Adam," Bryce said. "We all appreciate that you want to do everything you can for her. But if you give her even a couple pints of your blood, it will weaken you. And we have to be at our strongest to defeat Shaetore."

"I'm going to do it," Adam said. "I have to give her that chance."

"Ted got several transfusions," Sally said. "It didn't slow his latent bloodsucking tendencies down any."

"You don't know that," Adam said. "The transfusions may have bought him time."

"But in the end Ted still turned into a vampire," Bryce reminded him.

Adam spoke with emotion. "I can't just leave her

this way, don't you understand that? I won't leave her. Leave me if you have to."

"We're not going to leave you," Sally said patiently. "Where do you want to do the transfusion? You can't do it out here in the middle of the street."

"Maybe we should try to get back to the witch's castle," Bryce suggested.

"No," Adam said. "She already told us she couldn't help us with this battle. Besides, I have a better idea where to go."

"Where?" Bryce asked.

"To the end of the pier," Adam said.

"Why there?" Sally asked.

Adam glanced down at sleeping Watch. "It was Watch's opinion that vampires might be allergic to salt, since their blood rejects all the salt in their system as soon as they become vampires. I agree with that idea. I think the vampires will be reluctant to step onto the pier since they would then be surrounded by salt water."

"Being surrounded by salt water is not the same as being dumped in it," Bryce said. "Our being at the end of the pier probably won't slow them down one bit."

"It's just a theory," Adam agreed.

"Once we're at the end of the pier we'll have nowhere to run," Sally warned.

Adam glanced around at the dark night. He could sense dark shapes moving between the buildings. Crawling through the trees and maybe even flying through the air. In the distance, very clearly, he heard someone scream in pain and horror.

"Soon there will be nowhere left to run," Adam said out loud.

The beach area was deserted, which they took to be a good sign. Watch continued to sleep peacefully, and Cindy continued to stagger around spaced out. Yet none of them had forgotten how she had betrayed them in the cooler by shutting the door on them. She had started to lick her lips again, which also made them nervous.

Yet when they finally reached the end of the pier and laid Watch down on his back, it wasn't hard to coax Cindy into a kneeling position so she could accept a blood transfusion. Bryce knew a lot about first aid. It was he who set up the drip between Adam's vein and Cindy's. The whole time Cindy just stared out over the black sea. The surrounding salt water didn't seem to bother her, and Adam began to have doubts about his theory.

After a while he also began to wonder about giving Cindy his blood. He started to feel weak and dizzy, and a ringing noise grew in his ears. Sally and Bryce looked at him with concern.

"You have to stop," Bryce said. "You're getting too weak."

"And she's not getting any better," Sally said. "This is all useless."

Adam coughed weakly. "I have to keep trying." He tried to study Cindy in the night air, but her gaze was focused far off. "It might be helping her. A few minutes more."

"No," Bryce said, and removed the needle from Adam's arm. "Enough is enough. You're going to kill yourself for no reason."

"But . . ." Adam tried to protest.

"Don't argue with us," Sally said, removing the needle from Cindy's arm. If Cindy felt the needle going in or out, she gave no sign of it. Sally added, "I'm beginning to get nervous about where we are. I don't think a little salt water is going to stop Shaetore."

They heard a sound from the pier entrance.

Turning, they were stunned to see vampires approaching.

Dozens of them, Shaetore at their head.

They looked like an army of pale ghosts.

Except for their red eyes, which shone with an evil light.

guess you're right," Adam muttered. "What re we going to do now?"

"We're doomed," Bryce said bitterly.

Sally jumped up. "Maybe we can try reasoning with her. Explain to her that just because her mother was mean to her she doesn't have to drink our blood."

"That sounds like a brilliant strategy," Adam said sarcastically.

The guys got up when Cindy did. It seemed that their friend was still under the control of Shaetore, the blood transfusion notwithstanding. Cindy's eyes also shone with a red glow as the vampire queen drew nearer. Certainly Shaetore was not afraid of them. Thirty feet from the end of the pier she bid her followers halt. Then she stepped forward to meet them alone. Now she wore a long silver robe with a single large ruby hung around her neck on a silver chain. The jewel pulsed with a cold light. Shaetore had obviously recovered more quickly than Watch from the drugs they had absorbed. She smiled wickedly as she drew near.

"You have chosen a poor place to hide," she said. "And you should have known I could track you through her." She pointed to Cindy.

"We knew," Adam said. "We're just different from you. We don't discard friends for no reason."

Shaetore scowled. "Watch your words with me, young man. Your transformation into a vampire can be simple or it can be agonizing. You risk much in angering me."

"We don't care how angry you get," Sally snapped. "We heard about what you did to your uncle, Harome. He cared about you, and you sacrificed him to make yourself into the monster that you are."

Shaetore took a moment to reply.

Oddly enough, her expression was sorrowful.

"That was long ago," she said finally in a low voice. "In an age you know nothing about." Shaetore raised her hand. "Cindy, come to me."

As if in a trance Cindy moved forward.

"Cindy, no!" Adam shouted.

He tried to stop her, but she easily shook him off. She was very strong. Very pale.

Cindy took her place beside Shaetore. Behind Shaetore and Cindy the throng of vampires stirred restlessly. The queen glanced back at them, then at the gang.

"They want me to change you and be done with it," Shaetore said.

"Kill us," Adam said. "We would rather die human than live forever like you."

Shaetore smiled thinly. "I am not offering you a

. You are resourceful as mortals. You will be
n more resourceful as vampires. And in the days
to come I will need powerful servants."

Adam reached down and grabbed Watch's arms.
Quickly he pulled him to the edge of the pier.

"Adam!" Sally cried. "What are you doing?"

Adam continued to stare Shaetore down.

"We will jump and drown before we join you,"
Adam said. "We will never serve you and your evil
followers."

Shaetore seemed surprised. "You would give up
immortality for a principle?"

Bryce stepped to Adam's side.

"We live for our principles," Bryce said. "You will
not have us."

"But, guys," Sally whispered. "There are sharks
in these waters."

Adam remained resolute. "You will not change us
into vampires," he said. Shaetore continued to
regard him with amazement. Then her thin smile
widened.

"You bluff," she said. "You are afraid to jump."

"She might be right," Sally muttered.

"You called us heroes earlier," Adam said
proudly, getting a better grip on Watch's arms. He
intended to pull Watch into the black water below

with him. His dear friend would drown and never know why. Perhaps it was better that way, Adam thought. He continued, "We are heroes, and we aren't afraid of anything. Especially of a blood-drinking beast like you. You may have defeated us tonight, but you have not captured our souls. They are the one thing you can never take from us." Adam paused. "Ready to jump, Bryce?"

"Ready," Bryce said.

"Sally?" Adam asked.

Sally fidgeted. "I'm thinking."

Shaetore remained confident. "You won't do it. You are afraid. You are mere mortals. You have not lived long enough to—"

Shaetore did not finish.

Red blossomed on the chest of her robe, and she bent over in pain.

Cindy, stabbing from behind, had thrust a stake through her heart.

The horde of vampires shuddered.

Shaetore turned and stared back at Cindy in amazement.

Blood dripped from the vampire queen's mouth.

"How could you?" Shaetore gasped.

Cindy answered in a voice that sounded human. "I think it was Adam's blood," she said. "All the love he poured into it to try to save me. I have never killed anyone before, but I can kill you because you have no love left in you."

Shaetore struggled with the stake, without success. She was bleeding badly, dark blood. Her strength was failing.

"But I am your queen!" she cried.

"You are only a nightmare," Cindy said. Perhaps Cindy still had a measure of a vampire's strength left. With her last remark she suddenly shoved Shaetore toward the pier railing. For a moment the ancient queen looked as if she might recover her balance. But the wound Cindy had dealt her was too deep.

Shaetore fell into the dark water.

There was an explosion of red light and flame.

Crackling steam and smoke rose up toward the sky.

A thin cry followed.

There was so much pain in it, all their hearts were rent.

The horde of vampires suddenly seemed to be a group of ordinary people. Except for some of their clothes, which were definitely out of date. A tall thin man with a white beard slowly stepped forward. He wore a dull blue robe. There were tears on his face, but the gang couldn't tell if they were happy or sad ones. He paused when he reached Cindy and rubbed her head. Cindy appeared to be perfectly normal. The paleness of her skin had vanished when Shaetore died, and her eyes were now filled with human compassion. She, too, had tears on her face as she stared down at the water.

"I didn't want to kill her," Cindy said.

The man nodded his head as the others stepped up beside him. The old man stared at all of them and then wiped the tears from his face. His voice was kind and wise.

"I, too, wanted her to live forever," he said. "Perhaps that was my greatest mistake. Long ago I should have stopped her."

"But you didn't because you loved her," Adam said.

The old man nodded. "I loved her with all my heart."

"Are you Zy?" Sally asked, catching on at last.

"I was Zy," the old man said sadly as he stared down at the black water. There was no sign of Shaetore left. Not even ashes floating on the water. Zy continued, "Now I am no one. The curse is finally broken. All vampires have changed back into humans." He patted Cindy once more on the head. "Thanks to you."

The ancient wizard turned to leave.

"Where will you go now?" Adam called after him.

Zy paused and glanced over his shoulder.

"I don't know," he said.

Then he was gone, with the rest of those who had been vampires, some for only a day, others for centuries. Only one remained—Ted. He approached the gang as Watch finally began to stir and sit up. Ted patted Cindy on the back and shook his head in apology.

"I'm sorry I turned you into a vampire," he said.

"That's OK," Cindy said. "I won't hold it against you. I'm just happy we're well again."

Ted blushed shyly as if nervous.

He had quite a bit of blood in his cheeks.

"I was wondering if I could see you after all this settles down?" he asked Cindy. "I want to get to know you better."

Before Cindy could respond, Sally interrupted.

"Cindy," she said, "there is only one answer to that question when it comes from a guy who has previously changed you into a vampire."

"What's that?" Cindy asked.

Not, Sally said.

About the Author

Little is known about Christopher Pike, although he is supposed to be a strange man. It is rumored that he was born in New York but grew up in Los Angeles. He has been seen in Santa Barbara lately, so he probably lives there now. But no one really knows what he looks like, or how old he is. It is possible that he is not a real person, but an eccentric creature visiting from another world. When he is not writing, he sits and stares at the walls of his huge haunted house. A short, ugly troll wanders around him in the dark and whispers scary stories in his ear.

Christopher Pike is one of this planet's best-selling authors of young adult fiction.

LOOK FOR THE NEXT

SPOOKSVILLE™ #20

THE
DANGEROUS QUEST

by

Christopher Pike

COMING IN MID-DECEMBER 1997

From Minstrel® Books
Published by Pocket Books

SPOOKSVILLE™